Class No. ___5-8___ Acc No. ___C/2094S___

Author: ___Hoban, Russell___ Loc: ___2 AUG 1993___

___ 5 SEP 2002___

LEABHARLANN
CHONDAE AN CHABHAIN

1. This book may be kept three weeks. It is to be
   returned on / before the last date stamped below.
2. A fine of 20p will be charged for every week or
   part of week a book is overdue.

2 DEC 2002		
6 MAR 2003 / 4 JAN 2004		
4 JAN 2004 / 1 8 AUG 2004		
2 6 AUG 2006		
0 2 FEB 2007		
2 6 JAN 2008		

D0487565

JIM HEDGEHOG'S SUPERNATURAL CHRISTMAS

JIM HEDGEHOG'S SUPERNATURAL CHRISTMAS

HAMISH HAMILTON · LONDON

Leadarlanna
Conntae Cabain

Cavan County Library
Withdrawn Stock

Acc. No. 945
....No. J 5-8
Invoice Nº 875
Received £6.95

HAMISH HAMILTON LTD

Published by the Penguin Group
27 Wrights Lane, London W8 5TZ, England
Viking Penguin Inc., 40 West 23rd Street, New York, New York 10010, USA
Penguin Books Australia Ltd, Ringwood, Victoria, Australia
Penguin Books Canada Ltd, 2801 John Street, Markham, Ontario, Canada L3R 1B4
Penguin Books (NZ) Ltd, 182–190 Wairau Road, Auckland 10, New Zealand

Penguin Books Ltd, Registered Offices: Harmondsworth, Middlesex, England

First published in Great Britain 1989 by
Hamish Hamilton Ltd

Text copyright © 1989 by Russell Hoban
Illustrations copyright © 1989 by John Rogan

1 3 5 7 9 10 8 6 4 2

All rights reserved. Without limiting the rights under copyright reserved
above, no part of this publication may be reproduced, stored
in or introduced into a retrieval system, or transmitted, in any form
or by any means (electronic, mechanical, photocopying,
recording or otherwise), without the prior written permission of both
the copyright owner and the above publisher of this book.

British Library Cataloguing in Publication Data
CIP data for this book is available from the British Library

ISBN 0-241-12794-7

Printed in Great Britain by
BPCC Hazell Books Ltd
Member of BPCC Ltd
Aylesbury, Bucks, England

—1—

WAITING FOR THE BLOB

Jim Hedgehog liked to watch TV and he liked to eat. Every day when he got home from school he had a snack while he watched *Star Hog* and *Prickles* and *The Small Mammal Quiz*.

"You're always sitting in front of the TV and eating," said Dad.

"If I sit behind it I can't see anything," said Jim as he finished a salami and cheese sandwich and started a peanut butter and gherkin sandwich.

"Don't get any of that on the couch," said Mum.

"Not to worry," said Jim, "the bits that fall out are landing on my stomach."

"Have you done your prep?" said Dad,

"I always do it after *The Small Mammal Quiz*," said Jim as he finished the peanut butter and gherkin sandwich and peeled a banana.

"Why?" said Dad.

"I know more then," said Jim.

"You ought to get more exercise," said Mum.

"I've put my snack far away from me so I have to stretch for it," said Jim as he reached for a piece of chocolate cake.

"You're putting on a bit of weight," said Mum.

"I'm growing," said Jim.

"From front to back and sideways," said Dad.

Every Wednesday Jim watched *The Spike Squad*.
He liked the way they smashed cars and blew things
up with dynamite. He usually had crunchy snacks
with that, celery and carrots and apples and muesli
bars.

On Fridays he watched *Bad Guys from Beyond the Galaxy*, and while the bad guys were busy with lasers he was busy with leftover pizza or potato pancakes or toad-in-the-hole or whatever else he could find in the fridge.

Best of all Jim liked monster films. His favourite was *The Revolting Blob*. It was regularly shown on bank holidays, Easter, and Christmas and he was happy to see in the TV listings that this Christmas would be the same as always.

He remembered how cosy it had been last year staying up past his bedtime eating cold turkey and stuffing and cranberry sauce and plum pudding and trembling with fright while on the TV the Revolting Blob oozed along foggy streets belching and squelching and horribly rumbling.

He wrote cards and wrapped presents and helped to decorate the tree, and all the while he was looking forward to the evening of Christmas Day and the film.

—2—
NOW IT'S YOUR TURN

On Christmas morning Mum and Dad gave Jim the electronics lab kit he'd been wanting and he gave Mum a pair of earrings and Dad a pair of slippers.

Christmas dinner was wonderful as always and Jim had seconds and thirds of everything.

After dinner Mum and Dad and Jim went for a walk in the snow but they didn't stay out long because Jim had to make his preparations for watching *The Revolting Blob*.

"You don't want to eat too much before bedtime," said Mum.

"I won't," said Jim.

He loaded a tray with cold turkey and stuffing and cranberry sauce and plum chutney as well as a cold baked potato, peas and carrots and mixed salad, a loaf of French bread, a head of lettuce, a jar of mayonnaise, a jug of apple juice, and a pint of milk.

Also four clementines, some walnuts, a box of dates, and a thick slice of plum pudding.

He arranged everything within easy reach and settled down to watch the film.

At first the screen was dark and there was scary music as the title appeared in blob-shaped lettering.

Then came the credits and a little hedgehog walking home from school eating chips in a heavy fog on a dark winter day.

Every now and then the hedgehog stopped to look behind him.

There was a close-up of his face looking up.

Then the screen went dark and there was a horrendous belching and squelching and a dreadful rumbling. Jim grabbed the French bread and lettuce and mayonnaise and made a turkey sandwich with stuffing and cranberry sauce on the side.

The next scene was a deserted street late at night. The fog was so thick that the street lamps only made a feeble glow. Now there was no music, only a sound like the beating of a heart.

Something was coming but it wasn't visible yet. It was coming closer, closer, closer ... SUDDENLY here it was. Jim jumped back and ate the cold baked potato and the peas and carrots and salad without noticing.

There on the TV screen the Revolting Blob was looking straight at him.

"I don't remember this part," said Jim.

"I REMEMBER YOU, THOUGH," said the Blob. It had a voice like fifty tons of muck going slowly down the drain.

"You can't talk to me," said Jim. "You're not real, this is only a film."

"YOU'LL WISH IT WERE," said the Blob. "HAVEN'T YOU HEARD OF THE SUPER-NATURAL?"

"You're too fat to be supernatural," said Jim.

"I'M SUPERNATURALLY FAT," said the Blob. "WHAT ABOUT YOU?"

"I'm not fat," said Jim.

"HA HA," said the Blob. "I'VE BEEN WATCHING YOU FOR AS LONG AS YOU'VE BEEN WATCHING ME. YOU STARTED OUT THIN THE SAME AS I DID BUT YOU GOT FAT THE SAME WAY I DID. J GOT FATTER AND FATTER UNTIL I WAS SUPERNATU-RALLY FAT AND THAT'S WHEN I BECAME THE REVOLTING BLOB. DO YOU KNOW WHERE I LIVE?"

"I don't want to know," said Jim. He tried to back away but he couldn't take his eyes away from the Blob's eyes and he was being pulled closer and closer to the TV.

"I LIVE HERE IN THIS BOX AND I'M SICK AND TIRED OF IT," said the Blob. "NOW IT'S YOUR TURN." It reached out of the screen and pulled Jim into the TV without breaking the glass.

"Help!" shouted Jim, but Mum and Dad didn't hear him.

—3—

NO OTHER WAY

There was Jim inside the TV looking out at his own living room.

And there was the Revolting Blob oozing all over the couch and finishing up the turkey and the stuffing and the plum pudding and everything else.

"Help!" shouted Jim again. "Mum! Dad! Get me out of this!"

Mum and Dad came into the living room and saw the Revolting Blob oozing all over the couch.

"Jim," said Mum to the Blob, "I've told you many times not to get food all over the couch when you're watching TV."

"That isn't me!" screamed Jim from the TV. "That's the Revolting Blob! Can't you tell the difference?"

"How much longer are you going to be watching your film?" said Dad to the Blob.

"I don't really want to see any more," said the Blob in Jim's voice.

"Off you go to bed, then," said Dad. He switched off the TV and Jim couldn't see or hear what was happening in the living room after that.

He imagined the Blob kissing Mum and Dad goodnight and going upstairs to bed. "I DON'T BELIEVE THIS," he said, and the voice that came out of him was the voice of the Blob.

"Listen!" yelled someone behind Jim in the TV. "That's the Revolting Bob!" Somebody blew a whistle and Jim heard the sound of running feet coming towards him. He squelched away into the fog as fast as he could.

"It went that way!" they shouted behind him, and the footsteps came closer. Jim kept squelching until he came to a manhole cover. He lifted up the lid, oozed in, went a little way down a metal ladder, and pulled the cover back over the hole.

He couldn't see anything at all in the darkness, and as he listened he heard the footsteps stopping on the manhole cover. "I think it went down here," said a voice.

"Are you going after it?" said another voice.

"Not me," said the first voice. "I was only in the scene where the crowd chases the Blob. Nobody said anything to me about crawling down holes. Are you going down there?"

"Not likely," said the second voice, and the footsteps went away.

Jim waited until he thought it was safe, then he lifted the manhole cover and tried to ooze out. But now the hole was too small for him.

"I OOZED IN HERE," he said. "WHY CAN'T I OOZE OUT?"

"*Out?*" said his echo.

"OUT," said Jim. "I DON'T WANT TO SPEND CHRISTMAS DOWN A SEWER."

"*This isn't a sewer,*" said the echo.

"WAIT A MOMENT," said Jim. "IF YOU'RE AN ECHO WHY AREN'T YOU SAYING WHAT I SAY?"

"*What's the good of both of us saying the same thing?*" said the echo.

"YOU WERE SAYING THIS ISN'T A SEWER," said Jim.

33

"*That's right,*" said the echo. "*It's the thin way back.*"

"ISN'T THERE ANOTHER WAY?" said Jim.

"*The fat way got you in here,*" said the echo. "*Thin is the only way out. Do you want to give it a try?*"

"I HAVEN'T GOT MUCH CHOICE," said Jim.

"*Follow me,*" said the echo, "*and be ready to defend yourself at all times.*"

"AGAINST WHAT?" said Jim.

"*You know what,*" said the echo.

—4—
UNDER ATTACK

Jim oozed down the ladder and found the opening of a very narrow tunnel. It was so narrow that if he'd been any fatter he couldn't have got into it.

"ARE YOU DOWN HERE?" he said to the echo.

"*Down here!*" said the echo. "*Look out, commando attack!*"

Jim smelled something coming towards him. It was a smell he knew. "I'M NOT SURE I CAN HANDLE THIS," he said.

"*Handle this!*" said the echo.

"It's you or me," hissed a new voice in the dark, and a giant pizza leapt at Jim. It was his favourite kind, with salami.

He wanted to take a big bite but he knew that if he took even a little bite he wouldn't fit the tunnel any more. So he shut his mouth and rolled himself up tight.

"Open your mouth and fight like a Blob!" said the pizza.

But Jim kept his mouth shut and he rolled right through the pizza and kept on going.

"*From here on it gets dangerous*," said the echo as the
tunnel narrowed a little and went uphill. Very soon
Jim was out of breath. He was puffing and blowing
when the echo said, "*Enemy approaching!*"

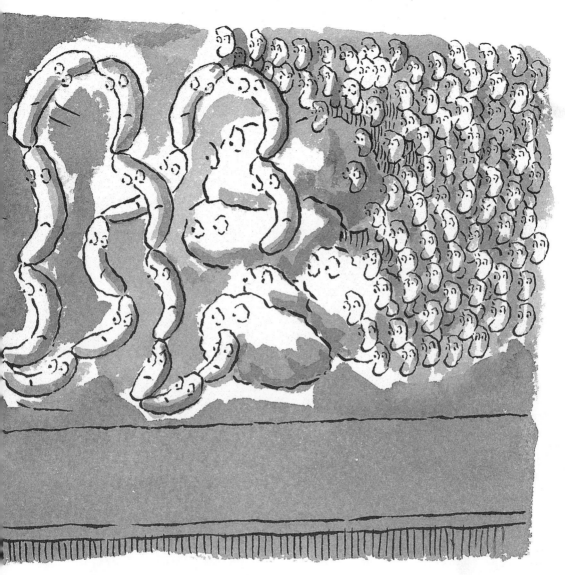

This time it was a company of bangers backed up by a battalion of mash with heavy baked-bean auxiliaries. They charged, yelling their battle cry, **"FAT IS GOOD!"**

"THIN IS THE WAY I'M GOING," said Jim.

He exploded the bangers harmlessly with his prickles, trod the beans into the mash, flattened the mash into patties, and pressed on without tasting a morsel.

All through the Christmas holiday Jim fought his way, through ever-narrowing tunnels in the super-natural darkness, below the foggy streets where the Blob had oozed. After a while he lost count of the days and the battles.

He was attacked by three-course meals and TV snacks and tiny nibbles. He was ambushed by appetisers, puddings, and innumerable leftovers. And while he got more and more tired, the enemy always had fresh troops to hurl at him.

—5—
YOU WIN

The final battle was on New Year's Eve, when a division of fanatical chocolate cakes launched a major offensive at midnight. **"EAT US!"** they screamed.

It was a grim and tight-mouthed Jim who battered them into little crumbs without taking a single bite or even a lick of the deliciously rich and creamy icing.

"*Well done!*" said his echo.

"Done?" said Jim, and he heard himself speaking in his own voice. The tunnel seemed very wide now and he thought he could see a dim light at the end of it.

He went towards it and found himself out in the open air in his own street. There was a full moon shining brightly on fresh snow. His house was all lit up and he could hear people singing 'Auld Lang Syne'.

Jim looked down at himself and saw that he was
covered with mozzarella cheese, mashed potatoes,
chocolate icing and many other tokens of the battles
he had fought. But he wasn't Blob-shaped any more.

He went round to his back door and sneaked up to his room. The bed was neatly made and there was a note on the pillow:

On New Year's morning Jim could tell by the way his parents acted that they'd never known he was gone. But they were surprised at how much weight he'd lost.

"How did you manage it?" said Dad. "All through the holidays you've been eating like a Revolting Blob and here you are looking quite thin."

"I made a supernatural effort," said Jim.

"'*Revolting Blob* II' is on TV today," said Mum. "I guess you'll be doing some heavy snacking with that one."

"Actually, I don't think I'll be watching any TV today," said Jim, and he went out jogging before breakfast.

CAVAN COUNTY LIBRARY